THE GRANDPA STORIES

Paul Breslin

VANTAGE PRESS
New York

To my dear daughter, Janet, who inspired me
to write these stories for my grandsons, Jason
and Kenton.

Illustrated by Jeff Mayes

FIRST EDITION

Copyright © 1997 by Paul Breslin

Published by Vantage Press, Inc.
516 West 34th Street, New York, New York 10001

Manufactured in the United States of America
ISBN: 0-533-12048-9

0 9 8 7 6 5 4 3 2 1

He traveled outlands
leaving strange places better
for his being there.
                    —Brezy

Contents

"Dad, I wish you'd write some stories for the boys," was my daughter's way of telling me to write something useful for a change. To my daughter, Janet, goes full credit for motivating me to do something I'd wanted to do since I retired in 1985. I'd dreamed of getting back to creative writing—to a luxury I'd sacrificed grudgingly to make a living as a young married man.

To my practical dad and my understanding mother go thanks for letting me dream-away my childhood while they kept busy supporting and nurturing their twelve children.

I acknowledge the help of my brother, Dan, and my sister, Barbara, who acted as consultants on two of the Grandpa stories; of other family members and friends who encouraged me with praise and corrections. Especially, do I acknowledge the help and encouragement of Betsy Greenstein of Wayland who asked many pointed questions and offered several productive suggestions.

THE GRANDPA STORIES

Grandpa and the Trolley Snow Plow

One of the stories "Grumps" told Jason and Kenton went way back to the time when their grandfather was a little boy. During a blizzard, he liked to look out the big front window of the house he grew up in. In those days, special gray-painted work trolleys had plow-blades like giant wings attached to their bays to clear the snowdrifts from the tracks along the avenue. Grumps told the boys he made believe those work trolleys were good-natured monsters that liked to help men fight bad-tempered winter storms.

One night, Grumps heard one of the plows growling in the fury of a blizzard. The snow had built up so high that, for all its might, the trolley plow could not clear the snowdrifts. "I must get through!" the trolley-plow repeated each time it backed up and smashed again into the freezing drifts. "What if there's a fire?" the trolley cried out. Even the great avenues were blocked after a blizzard if the trolley-plows couldn't clear the drifts.

Grumps watched the trolley-plow back up and crash again and again into the drifting snow that was beginning to pack as hard as a mountain of ice. "I must get through," the trolley-plow repeated each time it smashed into the rocklike drifts.

After two long hours, with the fury of the storm blowing and swirling at its worst, charging as fast as it could, with one tremendous effort, the plow crashed its way through the freezing snow mounds and cleared the avenue all the way to Davis Square, a mile away. "Now I'm not worried anymore," Grumps told the boys he heard the trolley-plow sigh. "If there is a fire, the engines will be able to get through."

The boys liked it when Grumps told them he always used to think about that trolley-plow whenever he had a big job to do.

Kenton, the Little Engine That Always Used to Break Down

"I can do that," Kenton, the little engine, always used to say. "Yes, I will haul another car across the country to help Santa get all his toys to the West Coast on time." But when he got to the Rocky Mountains, Kenton would always burst a pressure gasket and be unable to make it over the Rockies.

Mr. Calculate Stress, the train master, got fed up with what he called Kenton's need for recognition. "You've got to learn your limitations," he scowled, as he wrote the order to put Kenton in the car barn for repairs. While he was there, Kenton no longer held onto his first place of honor on the assignment list.

"I know! I know!" Kenton would assure Mr. Stress. But each time, he made the same mistake. "Yes, I can haul all those extra cars anywhere you wish," he'd insist. And the same thing would happen all over again. He would

break down and end up for repairs in the car barn at the busiest time of the year.

During the holiday rush last year, Mr. Stress wouldn't give Kenton a new assignment and Kenton spent the holidays all alone in the dreary car barn. He pouted about what little confidence Mr. Stress had in his ability to get the job done.

This year, however, Kenton went to Mr. Stress and told him, "I have learned my limitations. I can haul only five cars over the Rockies. If you let me do the job, I will get those five cars to the West Coast in record time."

It just so happened this year that Mr. Stress had only five cars leftover that the other engines couldn't haul over the Rockies. "If you get these five cars to the West Coast in record time, I will give you back your first place of honor on the assignment list," he promised Kenton.

That same night, Kenton took off for the West Coast. He did not start with a big show-off burst of power. This time he started with confidence at a strong, steady, even pace, thinking about the hard climb ahead. By the time he got to the Rockies, Kenton still had enough reserve power to haul his five-car load over the mountains as if he were climbing over an ant hill.

In record time, Kenton reached the West Coast where all the other engines cheered wildly for him. Mr. Stress telegraphed him congratulations for winning back his first place of honor on the assignment list.

Kenton had learned his limitations and soon became known as the most successful engine in the history of all the East Coast car barns.

The Land-of-Never-Disappoint

You could not get into the Land-of-Never-Disappoint without paying a border guard fifty dollars' worth of green tears for admission. Since Jason and his brother Kenton had never had that kind of money, they decided they would sneak across the border without paying the toll.

The Forest-of-Grappling-Trees and the River-of-Unavoidable-Tears were the biggest obstacles they would have to overcome. Life had designed these obstacles to keep non-paying customers out of the Land-of-Never-Disappoint. But Jason and his brother Kenton had made up their minds to get by them without paying one cent of green tears.

One of the grappling trees grabbed them up when they tried to get by him without paying the toll. "Hah! Hah!" scoffed the Grappling-Tree. "Now I have you in my grasp. What are you going to do about that?"

Being smart children, Jason and Kenton did nothing about being caught. Instead, they pretended to be helpless, until the Grappling-Tree went to sleep. Then they slipped out of the tree's grasp and headed for the next obstacle: the River-of-Unavoidable-Tears.

At the River-of-Unavoidable-Tears, Life had stationed an ugly ferryboatman with dirty, daggerlike teeth. "The toll here is fifty unavoidable tears, wiped dry and forgotten." The ugly ferryboatman clacked his dagger-teeth together when he demanded the toll from the boys.

"We never carry that kind of money," explained Jason, "but we want you to take us across the river anyway."

"No way! No way!" declared the ferryboatman, grinding his dagger-teeth with grim determination.

"If you don't take us across the river," threatened Jason, "my brother and I will pelt you with rotten apples until you give up. Come on, Kenton," he called to his brother to follow him to a nearby apple orchard where there were plenty of rotten apples lying on the ground.

Right away, Jason splattered the ferryboatman smack in the face with the biggest rotten apple he could find. Kenton managed only to splash his rotten apples all over the deck of the river ferry. Before long, however, the ferryboatman threw up his hands and hollered out through his dagger-teeth, "I surrender! I surrender! O.K.! O.K.! So I will take you both across the river without your paying one green cent of unavoidable tears."

It was so strange there. Jason and Kenton were very disappointed when they finally did reach the Land-of-Never-Disappoint. It kept raining torrents of black acid. There was no sunshine and the whole landscape, without vegetation, was dark and colorless. Nothing was growing there—not trees, not grass, and certainly not flowers. No birds were singing, either, as in their own back yard at home. Only songless black crows and cackling grackles flitted across the bleak sky or fought with each other for whatever little insects they could find to eat.

No sooner had Jason and Kenton experienced all this disappointment in the Land-of-Never-Disappoint than both of them wanted to go home. But they first had to earn $200 worth of green tears to get back across the River-of-Unavoidable-Tears and safely back through the Forest-of-Grappling-Trees.

For fifteen years, Jason and Kenton broke up huge boulders with heavy sledgehammers to make the crushed stone that Life needed to repair all its heavily-traveled roads. By the time they had earned enough toll money to pay their way safely back home, both of them were young men. They were old enough to know that the Land-of-Never-Disappoint was really the Land-of-Make-Believe. They were old enough now to know that that land had never really existed to begin with!

Neither Jason nor Kenton ever wanted to go back there again, anyway!

The Day Jason and Kenton Had the Most Fun in the Whole World

It was strange the way the sun came up that day. It didn't rise in the sky the way it usually does. This particular morning it rolled up like a big ball of fire over the trees in the boys' back yard.

"What do you want to do today, Kenton?" Jason sighed. School had been out for the summer only four weeks and already Jason was getting bored with all the free time he had on his hands.

"Let's take a balloon trip over the bay," suggested Kenton.

"That's silly!" scoffed Jason. "We don't have a balloon big enough to carry us. And even if we did, Mom wouldn't let us ride in it over the bay."

"We have a lot of little balloons. Let's fill them with the helium from Daddy's big tanks and tie them together," imagined Kenton who was always inventing things in his mind.

"Hey, that's a great idea!" shouted Jason, caught up with the adventure of it, "and we could use one of Mommy's big bed sheets to hold them all together like an up-side-down bag and use our red wagon with the high fence sides on it for a caboose." Jason didn't know the word *gondola*, but he could always come up with the necessary detail once his brother Kenton got a bright idea.

All morning, they worked out in the yard. It was hard tying tight the end of each balloon without losing any of the gas. The hardest part was getting their mother's big bed sheet over all the balloons and tethering securely the lively, bouncing mass of it to a nearby tree.

Kenton wondered out loud, "How will we tie the caboose-wagon to the end of it?"

"That's easy," explained his brother. "We'll just string four even clothesline ropes to a hole we'll drill in each corner of the cart."

Just as the sun was highest over their house, they heard their mother screaming, "This is the third time I've had to call you boys to come in for lunch. If you don't come in this instant, you'll find yourselves grounded—sitting all afternoon on the hallway stairs."

That word "grounded" in the boys' ears had an awful-threatening sound to it. Faster than she'd ever seen them respond before, their mother turned around from the stove to see them both sitting like two little angels at the family-room lunch table.

Right off, "What have you two boys been up to?" their mother wanted to know. Seemed whenever they looked like angels, they'd been up to something!

Jason kicked Kenton under the table. His brother was just about to explain the whole adventure to his mother. "Oh, we've been blowing up balloons and tying them together in bunches of different colors," Jason explained truthfully.

"That's nice!" their mother commented. It all sounded so harmless. She put two more pieces of bread in the toaster, because Kenton had already gulped down his toasted tuna sandwich in four or five bites . . .

It didn't take Jason long to drill a hole in each corner of their wagon "caboose." Quickly, he tied four even clothesline ropes to each corner of the wagon and tightly together around the tail of the sheet that held all the balloons together in one huge upside-down bag.

"We'll take water balloons for weights," he told Kenton, "When we want our balloon to go up, we'll toss a few water bags over the side of the caboose. When we want it to go down, we'll puncture one or two of the little balloons right through the sheet with this long stick with the nail taped on the end of it."

When they both were sitting inside the caboose, holding tight to the fence-sides of it, Jason ordered Kenton to throw two water bags over the side. But Kenton had no intention of letting go of his hold on the sides. "Oh, all right, then! I'll do it," Jason bravely decided.

Jason and Kenton had agreed quickly to call the balloon, "Adventure." Slowly, smoothly, "Adventure" began to lift off. Kenton's eyes were as wide as honey dew melons and his face was just as pale. Jason feigned bravado. He kept shouting, "I'm the captain! I'm the captain!" as if his little brother were in any state of mind to challenge his leadership.

It was an almost windless afternoon. They just seemed to drift over the yards of the two next-door neighbors. Just as they drifted over Jeremy Robust's yard at the end of Willow Street, however, the balloon started to sink down. A big dog came loping out of Robbust's mansion, barking his head off. A cook in white clothes and a floppy pastry hat, shaking a big wooden spoon, came chasing out after the barking dog.

As soon as they hit ground, Jason and Kenton rolled out of the caboose onto the lawn. The cook in the white clothes threw his big wooden spoon for the dog to chase after and grabbed the two boys by the scruff of the neck.

Two hours later, the boys' mother got a phone call from somebody asking her if she knew where her boys were. "Why, yes. Of course I know where my boys are! They're right out in the back yard, playing with balloons."

"They may be playing with balloons, all right," agreed the caller. "But they're in our front yard and, for all I know about it, they just dropped down right out of the sky."

The boys' mother didn't punish them that night after Mr. Robust's cook delivered them at the front door. "They could have dropped down in the bay and drowned," she explained to their father when he came home from work.

Before they went to sleep that night, both the boys had exactly the same thought: *Today was the best adventure we ever had in the whole world!* Before they knew anything else—this time, not like a big ball of fire—but like a gigantic red balloon, the sun had rolled up over the trees in their back yard again. The same idea occurred to both boys. *What a day for a great new adventure!* they thought.

The Day Jason and Kenton
Journeyed Under the Earth

Neither Jason nor Kenton had ever before
noticed this cave at the end of Willow Avenue.
But there it was, almost completely hidden
from view by dense bushes, its black mouth
gaping at them, daring them to enter and
explore.

"How far in do you think the cave goes?"
Jason asked his brother, as if Kenton had any
more information about this strange,
newly-discovered cave than he had.

"Probably to China," surmised his brother,
enlisting that wild imagination of his.

Without hesitation, always
adventuresome, the two boys began picking
their way slowly down the steep pathways of
the cave. About five hours later, they saw an
arrow-headed road sign that read: "To the
River Acheron."

Jason was helping Kenton by the hand
when he slipped. They both went sliding down

the longest natural chute they'd ever been on. Finally, they came to a sudden stop at the foot of another signpost. "Mt. Olympus, Greece, 100 miles above," it read.

It was dark in the cave but not so dark they couldn't see around the strange underworld into which they'd slid. Spooky evaporation clouds swirled up from a winding river about one hundred yards ahead of them. Right on the bank of the river stood a shaggy-bearded, wispy-haired old man holding a big oar beside what looked to them like a row boat drawn up on the river shoreline.

Jason wanted to know right off, "Will you take us across the river?" He'd gone over to the old man beside the boat. He didn't like the looks of all the ghostly figures he saw milling around.

"What are your names?" droned the old geezer, his glassy eyes peering off spookily through the swirling mist.

"I'm Jason. My brother's name is Kenton."

"I don't see either of your names on any list," muttered the old geezer, who told them his name was Charon. "That's what we get for letting that stupid three-headed mutt Cerberus keep the books for us! . . . By Mercury, I'll just write in your names myself to correct the record. How did you boys get here anyway?"

"We found a cave at the end of Willow Street in Southport."

"Southport . . . ? Never heard of it!"

"It's in Connecticut, in the United States of America," piped Jason who was studying geography in school.

"Never heard of 'em! What is this, anyway? Some kind of scam? I transport only qualified people on the Acheron who are headed for Hades."

"Is that a good vacation place?" inquired Jason.

"People who like sunlight prefer Elysium."

"Yeah, that's where we'd like to go. That's why we brought our sunglasses." Jason fished in his shirt pocket for his sunglasses.

"Before I can ferry you to Elysium, you will first have to go back to the sign 'To Mt. Olympus' and make the hard climb up from there. Without a burial certificate, besides a good record, you will have to pay the new gatekeeper a higher price for a pass to Elysium."

Jason and Kenton had found five gold coins on their journey down the cave pathways

and had pocketed them the same way they did pretty seashells at home. Before they would go back to the Mt. Olympus sign, however, Jason was curious to see what Hades looked like. He took two coins from Kenton and quickly paid Charon. "Before we cast off," said Charon, "you'll both have to drink some Lethe water."

Kenton—a very trusting boy—gulped down a whole cupful of Lethe water. Jason, however, remembering his mother's warning, "Never eat or drink anything a stranger offers you," only pretended to drink his water. He didn't like the way that with one hand Charon had waved his big oar menacingly in their direction while he held out his other hand for the coins. When Charon wasn't looking, Jason dumped the Lethe water down his shirt front. Turning to his brother, "You know what, Kenton?" he remembered. "Mom said if we are not home in time for supper tonight, we'll both have to sit for an hour on the hallway stairs."

"I forgot all about that!" gulped Kenton, groggily scratching his head.

"You keep the coins," Jason told Charon, generously. "We have to get back home in time for supper.

It's a good thing Jason hadn't drunk the Lethe water. He was able to remember the long way back up out of the cave and found footholds going up the chute. Otherwise, the boys would have been sitting for the rest of their lives of the hallway stairs!

Before they went to sleep that night, the boys plotted how someday soon they would explore again this strange underworld in search of Elysium. Having heard from their mother all they wanted to know about Hades, they agreed they did not want to end up in that place!

Glossary for *The Day Jason and Kenton Journeyed Under the Earth*

1. Acheron (Ak' a ran). River the dead had to cross to get to Hades.
2. Cerberus (Sur' ber us). Three-headed dog guarding Hades.
3. Charon (Ker' an). Boatman who ferried souls to Hades.
4. Elysium (i lizh' e am). Afterlife home of good souls who'd earned everlasting happiness. (*) Modern day = Heaven.
5. Hades (Had'ez). Place of the dead. Modern-day synonym for "Hell." More akin to modern-day idea of Purgatory.
6. Hades, Elysium, and Tartarus were separate regions of the same "underworld."
7. Lethe (Le-the). River of Forgetfulness in the underworld.
8. Mt. Olympus (O lim' pas). Home of the gods.